This book belongs to

_____

To my family: Mum, Dad, Pen, and Lin.
—A.C.

To my beautiful Miss Jane and family.
—L.F.

immedium

inspiring a world of imagination

Immedium, Inc.
P.O. Box 31846
San Francisco, CA 94131
www.immedium.com

First hardcover edition published 2009.

Edited by Don Menn
Book design by Luke Feldman aka SKAFFS

Printed in China
10 9 8 7 6 5 4 3 2 1

Library of Congress Cataloging-in-Publication Data

Chin, Amanda.
 Chaff n' Skaffs : Mai and the lost Moskivvy / by Amanda Chin and Luke Feldman;
illustrated by Luke Feldman. -- 1st hardcover ed.
   p. cm.
 Summary: A lost mosquito interrupts young Mai's sleep, and when she and her
friend Chaff decide to escort him back to his family, she gains self-confidence
as she ventures far from the comfort of her safe home.
 ISBN-13: 978-1-59702-013-8 (hardcover)
 ISBN-10: 1-59702-013-3
 [1. Self-confidence--Fiction. 2. Voyages and travels-- Fiction. 3.
Mosquitoes--Fiction.] I. Feldman, Luke. II. Title. III. Title: Chaff and
skaffs . IV. Title: Mai and the lost Moskivvy.
 PZ7.C44227Ch 2009
 [E]--dc22
                          2008039700

ISBN: 1-59702-013-3
ISBN 13: 978-1-59702-013-8

Chaff n' Skaffs

Mai and the lost Moskivvy

written by Amanda Chin and Luke Feldman
Illustrated by Luke Feldman

immedium
inspiring a world of imagination
San Francisco, California

Mai was a quiet girl who loved nature. She enjoyed watching the butterflies, bees, birds, and flowers. Yet she never ventured too far from home. Luckily her good friend Chaff always kept her company.

One day there was a big storm, and they heard the raindrops drum against her window.

On such days, Mai and Chaff read books, listened to music, played games, and painted in her bedroom.

That night whilst dreaming in bed, Mai was awoken by a loud "Bzzz!" The noise darted and dived about her in the darkness. She turned on her lamp and spotted a confused critter hovering by the wall.

BZZZZZZ

The restless mosquito was soaked from the rain. But try as she might, Mai could not corral her guest who buzzed out of reach. Mai put a pillow over her head and tried to go back to sleep.

In the morning, Mai found the tired creature slumped on her bedside table. She gently placed the bug on the windowsill, so he could fly away. Yet he wouldn't budge.

She said, "G'day! My name is Mai and this is my friend Chaff. What is your name?"

"I'm Moskivvy," he replied. "Thanks heaps for your hospitality. I'm from the land of Skaffs."

"I'm afraid you're lost," answered Chaff. "Skaffs is very far from here, way beyond the Gembrook Forest."

Mai froze at the thought of the nearby woods, which she had always been too scared to enter. The howling wind, the ghostly gum trees, and the glaring night eyes frightened her.

Shaking the thought away, Mai asked, "How did you get here?"

Moskivvy explained, "Yesterday I was playing amidst the dandelions with my brothers and sisters. Suddenly a storm approached, and my parents called us home.

I couldn't outrace the rain, so I grabbed onto a stem. But a gust of wind blew me high into the clouds."

"Like a feather I drifted up and away. Later, when I floated to the ground, I realized I was alone.

Through the trees, I saw your bedroom light and flew towards it," recalled Moskivvy. "I miss my family terribly. Can you help me get back home?"

Mai hesitated, since she didn't want to leave the comforts of home. However, Chaff whispered, "I'll protect you."

Feeling more confident with Chaff by her side, Mai agreed, "We'll bring you back, Moskivvy."

Their small pal was most grateful and together the team prepared for their journey.

Mai told her parents she was going out for a walk. But, in truth, she did not know when she'd return. Through the early morning mist, the trio set off west to the dark Gembrook Forest, where Moskivvy first landed. There Mai was surprised by what she saw.

The sun's warm rays filtered
through the trees and the floating
leaves. Families of wallabies,
koalas, and cockatoos came out
to greet them. Soon Mai forgot
her fear of leaving home.

Beautiful butterflies and buzzing bees bounced amongst the fragrant blossoms.

"I remember that Willow tree with bright red flowers," recalled Moskivvy. "We must be heading in the right direction."

They skipped along and noticed a bunch of creatures flying overhead. Could it be Moskivvy's family? Eagerly, Mai climbed the nearest tree.

Chaff stood below just in case. Reaching the insects, Mai petted them sweetly. "Sorry, these are lady bugs," she reported.

Continuing onwards, Mai spotted a cave. Could Moskivvy's family be in there? Chaff moved a boulder to widen the entrance and soon many strange eyes peered out at them. Mai turned to Moskivvy who was petrified!

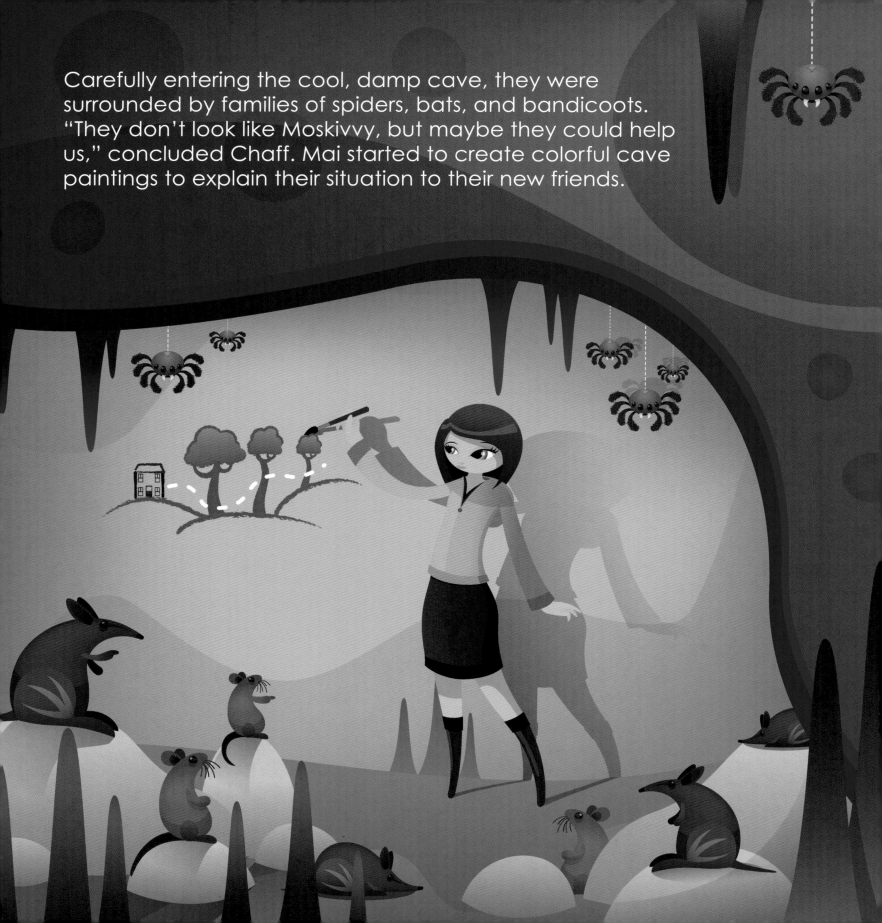

Carefully entering the cool, damp cave, they were surrounded by families of spiders, bats, and bandicoots. "They don't look like Moskivvy, but maybe they could help us," concluded Chaff. Mai started to create colorful cave paintings to explain their situation to their new friends.

The cave dwellers pointed to a light up ahead. As the opening got closer, the air grew colder. "Bzzz!" shivered Moskivvy and the noise echoed through the tunnel.

Mai suggested, "Maybe we should turn back."

But Chaff reminded Mai, "We must press on for Moskivvy's sake. His family surely misses him."

They emerged into a frosty white world. Trudging slowly forward, they encountered a snowstorm that whirled around them. Lost in the blizzard, Mai huddled next to Chaff and cried, "Which way now?"

Suddenly Moskivvy pointed south to a mountain. Sitting on the summit was a red temple, where music gently drifted down towards them. The soothing melody calmed Mai and coaxed them to climb the steep stairway.

At the top, the weary travelers were surprised to meet monks who welcomed them into their home. Chaff, Mai, and Moskivvy were relieved to find shelter and rested their feet inside the incense-filled room.

The guests sat at a festive table and gladly shared warm tea and a hearty feast. All the while, families of lively limas and groovy geckos entertained them.

Following the monks' advice, the refreshed explorers descended the mountain and headed east towards the Skaffs Sea.

The trio followed the sound of waves crashing against the rocks. "We must cross the water," Moskivvy decided. Mai had never been in a boat before and began to fret.

"No worries, Mai. I have sailed many seas before," whispered Chaff. They borrowed a boat and set off amidst a high tide and darkening sky. Mai gripped the sides of the vessel as Chaff hummed a comforting tune.

For what seemed like hours, they sailed the bubbling seas until they came to an inlet. In the shallow water the boat got bogged down, so they set out on foot to continue. "I remember playing here...we must be getting closer," Moskivvy noted as they waded north.

The scenery was more dazzling than any that Mai had read of in a book. Beside beautiful water lilies and elegant egrets, she tiptoed through the silvery stream. Looking up, Mai noticed the sky filled with little winged creatures. Could this be Moskivvy's family?

Spotting familiar faces, Moskivvy grinned as a joyous "Bzzz" surrounded the threesome. "Go on, what are you waiting for?" encouraged Mai and her eager companion zipped away.

Soon Moskivvy was hugged by happy relatives. "Are you ok?" cried his mum.

"Where did you go?" asked his dad.

"We missed you, mate!" exclaimed his siblings.

"Thank you so much," his parents said to Mai and Chaff. "Will you stay to celebrate Moskivvy's return?"

They agreed and enjoyed dancing and dining with the whole family.

But as the sun set, Mai became homesick. "Now my parents must be worried about me," she sighed. "How will I ever get back to my family?" Chaff held her hand as everyone wondered what to do.

"I have an idea," shouted Moskivvy. A cloud of mosquitoes swarmed around Moskivvy as he brainstormed. Next, in a flurry of movement they gathered materials to build something. "What is that odd contraption?" Chaff wondered.

Moskivvy's family had turned an old mosquito net into a flying trapeze!
"The least we can do is swing you back home," the mosquitoes cheered.

"That's pretty spiffy!" laughed Mai and quickly they lifted off.

With the wind in their hair, Mai and Chaff remembered all the places they had been. "Look below!" yelled Chaff, and they waved to the many friends they had made along the way.

Seeing her bedroom light, Mai called, "There's my house!" The mosquitoes gently lowered their passengers to the ground.

Gazing out their window, Mai and Chaff said farewell to Moskivvy. They all looked forward to a good night's sleep and to dreaming about more adventures to come.